Pearl and Wagner
One Funny Day

Kate McMullan • *pictures by* R. W. Alley

DIAL BOOKS FOR YOUNG READERS

For Kylie Mae Pearson
—K.M.

For Helene and Reuben, no kidding
—R.W.A.

DIAL BOOKS FOR YOUNG READERS ★ A division of Penguin Young Readers Group ★ Published by The Penguin Group ★ Penguin Group (USA) Inc., 375 Hudson Street, New York, NY 10014, U.S.A. ★ Penguin Group (Canada), 90 Eglinton Avenue East, Suite 700, ★ Toronto, Ontario, Canada M4P 2Y3 (a division of Pearson Penguin Canada Inc.) ★ Penguin Books Ltd, 80 Strand, London WC2R 0RL, England ★ Penguin Ireland, 25 St. Stephen's Green, Dublin 2, Ireland (a division of Penguin Books Ltd) ★ Penguin Group (Australia), 250 Camberwell Road, Camberwell, ★ Victoria 3124, Australia (a division of Pearson Australia Group Pty Ltd) ★ Penguin Books India Pvt Ltd, 11 Community Centre, Panchsheel Park, New Delhi - 110 017, India ★ Penguin Group (NZ), 67 Apollo Drive, Rosedale, North Shore 0632, New Zealand (a division of Pearson New Zealand Ltd) ★ Penguin Books (South Africa) (Pty) Ltd, 24 Sturdee Avenue, Rosebank, Johannesburg 2196, South Africa ★ Penguin Books Ltd, Registered Offices: 80 Strand, London WC2R 0RL, England

The art was created using pen and ink, watercolor,
and a few colored pencils on Strathmore Bristol.

CONTENTS

Wagner stayed up late reading.

The next morning, he did not hear his

alarm clock.

"Wagner!" called his mom. "Up, up, up!"

Wagner ate breakfast fast.

He grabbed his backpack

and raced to school.

No one was out on the playground.

He was late!

What would he tell Ms. Star?

Wagner zoomed down the hallway.

He saw Pearl at the drinking fountain.

"Guess what," said Pearl. "Ms. Star

is roller-skating around the classroom."

"She *is*?" said Wagner. He tried to

picture his teacher on roller skates.

Pearl started laughing.

"April fools!" she said.

"What?" said Wagner.

"Today is April Fools' Day," said Pearl.

"And I fooled you."

"Oh," said Wagner.

Wagner waited while Pearl got her drink.

They walked into the classroom together.

Ms. Star said, "Class, hand in your homework."

"Homework?" said Pearl.

"Uh-oh," said Bud.

Wagner started pulling everything

out of his backpack.

"April fools!" said Ms. Star.

Everyone laughed.

Everyone but Wagner.

He stuffed everything back into his pack.

At library time, Wagner took back his book.

"This book is overdue," said Mr. Fox.

"You owe a big fine."

"I do?" said Wagner.

"April fools!" said Mr. Fox.

"Oh, brother," said Wagner.

At lunch time, Pearl and Wagner

walked into the cafeteria together.

"I love April Fools' Day," said Pearl.

"Not me," said Wagner.

They stopped to read the menu.

"Ew!" said Pearl.

"Yuck!" said Wagner.

"Bug juice sounds good," said Henry.

"How about some fish-eye stew?"

asked Mr. Milk.

"I feel sick," said Wagner.

"April fools!" said Mr. Milk.

"What, no bug juice?" said Henry.

After lunch, Ms. Star said, "Clear your desks.

I will pass out the math test."

"April fools!" shouted Wagner.

"Sorry, Wagner," said Ms. Star. "It's for real."

She put a test on his desk. "You have

half an hour."

"Phooey!" said Wagner. "This is not my day!"

Chapter Two
THE DANCE CONTEST

"It's raining outside, class," said Ms. Star.

"Go down to the gym for recess."

"I have a surprise for you,"

said Mr. Jumper, the gym teacher.

"We are going to have a rainy-day

dance contest."

"Yippee!" said Pearl. "I am a great dancer."

"Oh," said Wagner. He was not so sure

about dancing.

"Pick a partner," said Mr. Jumper.

"Want to be partners?" said Wagner.

"Not right now, Wag," said Pearl.

"April fools, right?" said Wagner.

"No," said Pearl. "For real."

Pearl ran over to Bud.

"Want to be partners?" she said.

"Let's boogie!" said Bud.

Wagner was steamed.

He ran over to Lulu.

"Want to be partners?" he said.

"Are you a good dancer?" asked Lulu.

"Are you kidding?" said Wagner.

"I am the greatest."

"We'll go first!" called Pearl.

Mr. Jumper turned on his boom box.

"Let's jitterbug!" said Bud.

Bud twirled Pearl. Pearl twirled Bud.

Bud did the splits. Pearl jumped over him.

They danced like crazy.

When the music stopped,

everybody cheered.

Everybody but Wagner.

25

"Our turn!" said Wagner.

Mr. Jumper started up the music.

"Let's hip-hop!" said Lulu.

"Cool!" said Wagner.

He hopped in a circle.

"No, Wagner!" said Lulu. "Like this!"

Lulu tapped her feet to the beat.

She boogied on down.

She did some smooth moves.

"Now you try it," said Lulu.

"Okay," said Wagner.

Wagner tapped his feet.

But he could not find the beat.

He boogied on down and

fell on his behind.

"Dancing!" said Wagner. "Double phooey!"

And he stomped off.

Lulu ran over and grabbed Bud.

Bud and Lulu boogied on down.

They did some smooth moves.

Henry came over to Wagner.

"I can't dance either," Henry said.

He handed Wagner a cup. "Have some juice."

"Thanks," said Wagner. He took a big drink.

"What is this stuff?" asked Wagner.

"Bug juice," said Henry. "I made it myself."

"April fools?" said Wagner.

"No," said Henry. "For real."

"Yech!" said Wagner. "This is *not* my day!"

Mr. Jumper gave the prize to Pearl and Bud.

Then he turned up his boom box.

"Everybody dance!" he said.

And everybody did.

Everybody but Wagner.

"Silent reading time," said Ms. Star.

Everybody opened a book.

Wagner slumped down in his seat.

He held his tummy and groaned.

33

"Are you sick?" asked Pearl.

Wagner nodded.

Pearl raised her hand. "Ms. Star?" she said. "Wagner doesn't feel good."

"Do you want to go to the nurse?"

asked Ms. Star.

Wagner nodded.

He walked slowly to the door.

"Feel better, Wag!" called Pearl.

After a while, Wagner came back.

"Wagner!" cried Pearl.

"You are covered in spots!"

"Am I?" said Wagner.

His voice was so soft

Pearl could hardly hear him.

"What did the nurse say?" asked Ms. Star.

"I have a fever," said Wagner.

"And a bad case of bug pox."

"Is it catching?" asked Henry.

"Only if I sneeze," said Wagner.

"Ah-ah-ah-choo!"

Everyone jumped up and

ran away from Wagner.

He sneezed again, even louder:

"Ah-ah-AH-CHOO!"

"Stop it!" cried Lulu.

"Cover your mouth!" cried Pearl.

"Go home to bed!" cried Bud.

Wagner staggered forward.

He opened his mouth very wide:

"Ah . . . ah . . . ah . . . .

"... April fools!" shouted Wagner.

And he laughed himself silly.